Dear Donald Trump

For Emile, Oliver and Lilka, who all know
what it's like to share a room! – SS

For Willian, Nathan, Alexis and Maxime – AV

This edition first published 2018
Millwood Press, PO Box 28079
Havelock North, Hawke's Bay, New Zealand

Designed by Vida & Luke Kelly Design
Printed in China by Everbest Printing Co Ltd,
an accredited ISO 14001 and
FSC certified printer

ISBN 978-0-473-43281-2

Read more about our books at www.millwoodpress.net

Dear Donald Trump

Sophie Siers
Anne Villeneuve

MILLWOOD PRESS

NEW ZEALAND

Dear Donald Trump,

I'm writing you a letter from my bedroom in New Zealand.
Sadly, the room does not belong only to me. I have to share
it with my big brother who exactly fits your description
of an undesirable person.

I watched you on the TV news tonight and you said
you were building a wall. It made me think that perhaps
I need one too.

Yours faithfully,

Sam

Dear Donald Trump,

The problem is that my brother has a phone and he plays on it at night even though he isn't allowed. It keeps me awake. I suggested to Mum and Dad that they let me build a wall across the room.

They said no.

Very sincerely,

Dear Donald Trump,

At dinner tonight we had a discussion about the wall proposals, both yours and mine. I don't know about you but I'm getting a lot of negative feedback.

My brother said that they're both dumb ideas.

Mum said that if you were like other men she knew you would talk about it a lot but never build it.

Dad didn't say anything.

Respectfully,

sam

Dear Donald Trump,

Everybody was talking about your wall at school today.
There didn't seem to be many kids who thought it was a good idea.

They obviously don't know what it's like to share a room.

Our teacher, Mr Green, has set us a project on 'Great Walls of the World'. He said that some of them didn't quite work to plan. I told him that mine definitely would!

Yours truly,

Sam

Dear Donald Trump,

Dad took my brother and me fishing today.
He wanted to talk about the wall.

He said we needed to talk things over and see if we could "negotiate" a way to make things work in our room. I told him that actions speak louder than words.

I thought that's the sort of thing you'd say in my situation.

Best regards,

sam

Dear Donald Trump,

I've discovered I'm great at building walls! I've built two in the garden and one that went right across the pond which made a dam as well. I made them out of sand and stones and Dad said my best one looked like the Great Wall of China!

He told me that it was the biggest wall ever made and was built to hold back marauding invaders.

It sounds like just what I need.

Your friend,

Dear Donald Trump,

My brother is behaving like a marauding invader.
This morning he took my Star Wars destroyer.
That means war.

I told my mum that this could have been averted
if she had let me build a wall but she just LAUGHED!

I bet no one is laughing at y̲o̲u̲r̲ wall idea.

Good night from,

SAM

Dear Donald Trump,

I borrowed some books from the library to help me with
my wall project. The Great Wall of China is humongous!
Mum's favourite is the really old one in Zimbabwe.
Hadrian's Wall, which went right across England,
was 135 kilometres long!

My room is only 4 metres across — I don't understand
why it's such a big deal.

Yours frustratedly,

SAM-

Dear Donald Trump,

At school today my best friend, Robert Burns, told me you could see The Great Wall of China from space but Bella said that wasn't true.

I think I'll be an astronaut when I grow up, then I can see for myself.

Did you want to be a wall builder when you were a kid?

All the best,

SAM

Dear Donald Trump,

I stayed with my grandma this weekend. It's great staying there because I get my own room and Gran lets me do pretty much whatever I want.

The downside was that there were some strange noises in the night. I lay awake counting the walls between my room and Gran's.

. . . . 4 . . . . 5 6

There's six. I counted them a lot of times.

Ciao for now,

Dear Donald Trump,

There has obviously been some 'dialogue' while
I was away. My brother is using words like 'harmony'
and 'spirit of sharing' and suggesting that a wall
is not needed.

I, however, remain unconvinced.

Laters,

-SAM

Dear Donald Trump,

I'm still the only one in the house who thinks
that the wall is a good idea.

I'm committed to getting it done even if my big brother did 'ask' to borrow my pocket knife (he's <u>never</u> asked before) and last night he even went under the covers to use his phone!

Best,

Sam

Dear Donald Trump,

I'm having second thoughts about the wall.
Yesterday, my brother put my clean washing on my bed
(he usually dumps it on the floor). I said thank you and
returned the cap I borrowed from him a few weeks ago.
Things are much better.

At dinner Dad said he was proud of us and told a very
long story about a wall in Berlin that got knocked down.
He said that communication and negotiation are always
preferable to separation.

I kind of see what he means.

See ya,

Dear Donald Trump,

I'm really sorry but I'm dropping the whole wall idea.
To cut a long story short, a big brother in your room is
pretty cool when you've just had the worst nightmare ever.
I'm glad I hadn't got round to building it.

I feel a bit silly changing my mind but my brother says it's cool and Mum said she admires a man who admits when he's wrong.

Dad didn't say anything.

Anyway good luck with your wall.
Perhaps a small one would do?

Best wishes,

sam.